KU-360-037

SOUTHWARK LIBRARIES

SK 2869018 4

Awake or dreaming,
this book belongs to:

For Dri, who shares my dreams

∽ S.T.

To my babies' grandparents, who have been an amazing help –
gifting me with the time to immerse
myself in Sean's beautiful text

∽ A.A.

The Dream Train
Poems for Bedtime

SEAN TAYLOR   illustrated by ANUSKA ALLEPUZ

WALKER BOOKS
AND SUBSIDIARIES
LONDON · BOSTON · SYDNEY · AUCKLAND

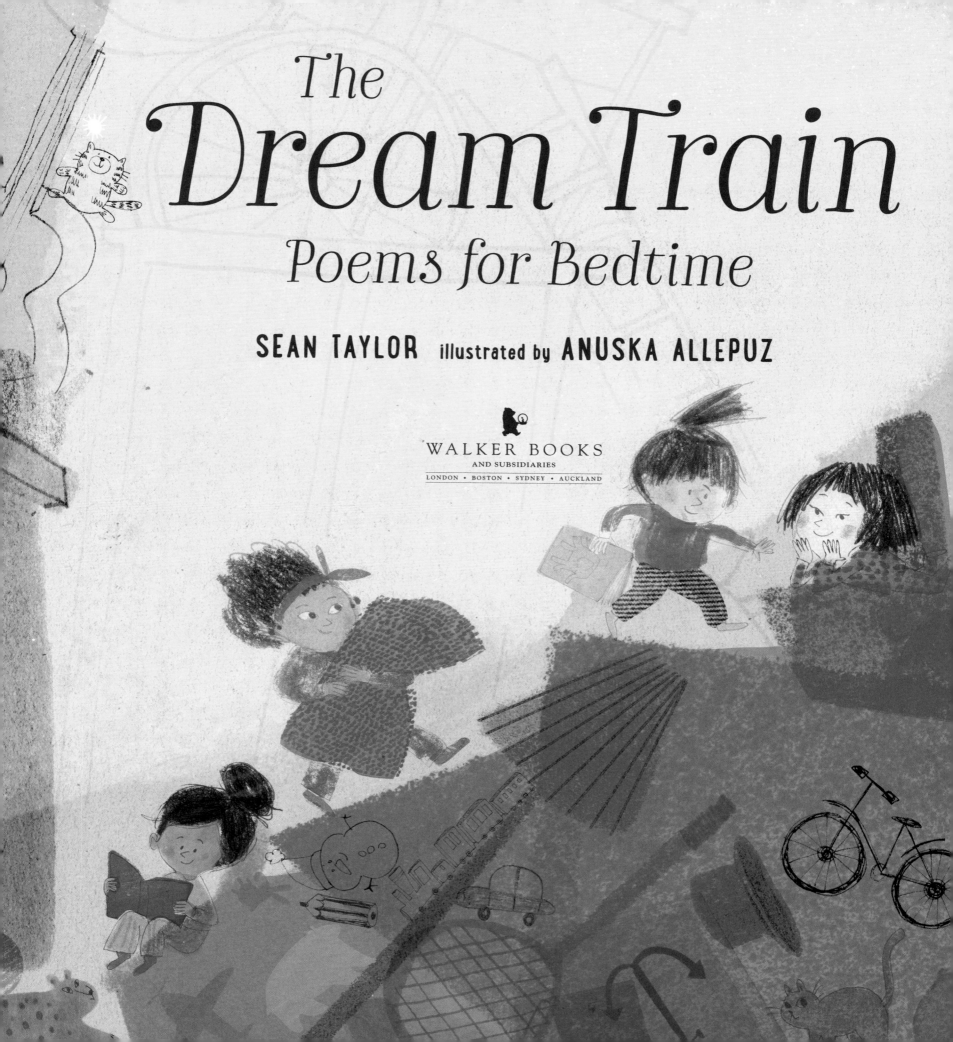

When you wake, you shall have
All the pretty little horses.

Dapples and greys, blacks and bays
All the pretty little horses.
Traditional lullaby

CONTENTS

DREAM WHEELS TURNING

NIGHT ARRIVES

HERE COMES THE NIGHT

Here comes the night.

Here come the birds,
swooping home.

Here comes the night.

Here comes darkness,
touching the birds
swooping home.

Here comes the night.

Here comes a boy
back with his mum.
Here comes darkness,
touching the birds
swooping home.

Here comes the night.

1

Here comes a star,
in the eyes of the boy
back with his mum.
Here comes darkness,
touching the birds
swooping home.

Here comes the night.

2

THE FUTURE

I can see the future.
I can see it in my head.
It's seven o'clock, so the future is ...

have a bath,
put on pyjamas,
brush my teeth,
and GO TO BED!

DUCKS LIKE TO DREAM

Ducks like to dream
for a while, on a pool.

Ducks love a doze.
Ducks think sleeping is cool.

Lions like to slumber,
stretched in the shade.

Lions love a kip.
Lions think sleeping is great.

Seals like to find
a smooth rock for a rest.

Seals love a snooze.
Seals think sleeping is best.

But squirrels think sleeping
is totally dumb.

Squirrels hate a nap.
Squirrels think jumping off
bouncy branches
is loads more fun.

ONE NIGHT

It
was
great
when we
stayed up
late, one night
in the summer
by the sea.
No one else was
there except the moon,
my dad, and me.
We were laughing
and running, because
everything felt
big and free.
And the moon
joined in the fun.
Its light jumped
for joy
on the
sea.

WHAT COMES?

What comes between
the day and the night?

What's made of darkness
but made of light?

What's almost dim
but almost bright?

Twilight.

9

RUN FREE

All day long,
working things out.

Then it's night-time –
minds run free.

All day long
questioning, answering.

Then it's bedtime –
minds run free.

All day long,
thinking thoughts.

Then dreams come –
minds run free.

STORY TIME

When night arrives, listen.

Right round the world,
you will hear it...

When night arrives, listen.

Wherever there are children,
you will hear it...

When night arrives, listen.

Right round the world,
you will always hear it.
Wherever there are children,
you will always hear it ...
the soft music of story time.

13

NIGHT SKIES

Moonrise. Bat flies. Night skies. Sleepy sighs.

Teddy eyes. Beddy-byes. Lullabies. Shut your eyes.

Sleepy sighs. Night skies. Bat flies. Moonrise.

16

WE'RE DIFFERENT

Mechanics know all about engines.
Children know all about games.
Gardeners put out seeds.
Fire-fighters put out flames.

A painter uses a brush.
A hairdresser uses a comb.
Nurses help you get better.
Tram drivers help you get home.

People are never the same.
We're different, it has to be said.
But one thing is true about all of us –
everyone goes to bed!

ONCE THERE WAS

The day is done.
Darkness comes.

Once there was a lake.
Now there's a mirror for the stars.

SHUT-YOUR-EYES TIME

G'NIGHT CAPTAIN

When my mum
turns off the light,
sometimes she smiles
and says, "G'night Captain!"

If she does,
I find I'm wearing
a captain's hat,
and my bed's a boat, with a sail.

Sometimes I pass
through the wild winds
and high-jumping waves
of a storm, miles out at sea.

23

Sometimes I sail
to faraway islands
and drift so close,
I hear the sounds in the trees.

But when my bed's
a boat, I'm safe.
It keeps me floating
however the sea may rock'n'roll.

That's why I like it
whenever my mum
turns off the light
and says, "G'night Captain."

24

EVERYONE

When it's lights-out,
if you lie there
feeling alone
in your bed,
in the gloom.

Just remember that,
in a way,
everyone who loves you
is there
in the room.

THANK YOU

Thank you, Today,
for the good things you gave me.
Thank you for the food,
the fresh air and fun.

And thank you, Tomorrow,
for always being there.
You're like a story
that no one's ever heard.

27

THE SLEEP STEALERS

The Sleep-Stealers' feet
are light and sure.
They tap on the window
and rattle the door.

And, just when your eyes
fill with flickers of sleep,
they'll set off a car-alarm
out in the street.

The Sleep-Stealers carry
a bag full of worry.
They empty it out,
then off they all hurry.

They'll make you cold.
They'll make you hot.
They'll give you an itch
that just won't stop.

But the Sleep-Stealers aren't
so tricky to beat.
There's no need for
lullabies or counting sheep...

Just close your eyes,
snuggle your feet,
think of your dreams,
and breathe deep.

Close your eyes,
snuggle your feet,
think of your dreams,
and breathe deep.

Close your eyes,
snuggle your feet,
think of your dreams,
and sleep.

THE BLANKET

The blanket Grandma knitted is
as green as a tree.

I used to see her clever fingers
knitting it for me.

The blanket Grandma knitted is
warm and thick.

Dad says there's a little bit
of love in every stitch.

The blanket Grandma knitted
helps me sleep at night.

I'm sure it sometimes whispers
"Good night, love. Sleep tight."

34

RAIN, RAIN, RAIN

Rain,
rain,
rain on the windows.

Rain on the rooftiles
over my head.

Rain,
rain,
rain again.

As I lie warm
and dry in bed.

Pitter patter. Spitter spatter.
Spitter spatter. Pitter patter.

Rain,
rain,
rain falling down.

Rain filling puddles,
ponds and streams.

Rain,
rain,
rain again.

Watering the plants, the trees
and my dreams.

Pitter patter. Spitter spatter.
Spitter spatter. Pitter patter.

36

If you'd like a good night's rest,
you'll find this advice is wise.

IS WISE

When you go to sleep ... don't forget to close your eyes.

ASKED BY A PILLOW

How many bricks
in a city?

How many fish
in a lake?

How many ticks
in a clock?

How many twists
in a snake?

How many threads in a cloth?

How many notes
in a flute?

How many raindrops
in a storm?

How many leaves
in a forest?

How many footsteps
in a boot?

How many flights
in a kite?

How many words
in a library?

How many dreams
in a night?

GRANDPA'S GUITAR

Normally there's the sound of
footsteps on the pavement,
or shop-shutters pulled in the dark.

But tonight,
in bed,
what I can hear
is the sound of
Grandpa's guitar.

Normally there's the sound of
cats fighting,
or the neighbours starting their car.

But tonight,
in bed,
what I can hear
is the sound of
Grandpa's guitar.

HUSHABYE TIME

The only things still moving
are clouds passing the stars.
Off they travel, high above
dark streets and quiet cars.

*And it's tucked-in-tight time,
say-goodnight time.*

All the day has passed.

*It's shut-your-eyes time,
say-goodnight time,
hushabye time, at last.*

Everything is quiet
except two whispering trees.
And soon they will be silent, too,
left by the last of the breeze.

Because it's tucked-in-tight time,
say-goodnight time.

All the day has passed.

It's shut-your-eyes time,
say-goodnight time,
hushabye time, at last.

DREAM
WHEELS
TURNING

THE DREAM TRAIN

Can you hear the dream train coming?

**CHUGGA! CHUGGA!
CHOO-CHOO-CHOO!**

Can you hear it, right on time,
coming down the tracks for you?

Can you see the dream train stopping?

CHUGGA..........CHUGGA.........
CHOO-CHOO................CHOO!

Now's your chance to climb on board
and find out where it's going to.

48

Can you feel the dream wheels turning?

CHUGGA! CHUGGA!
CHOO-CHOO-CHOO!

Off you go into the distance,
on a dream train, just for you.

50

JOANNA'S SLEEPING TIGHT

On the back seat of the car,
Joanna's sleeping tight.

What are you dreaming, Joanna,
as we travel through the night?

Are you dreaming big ...

of climbing through towering trees
and reaching up, up, up,
to catch their golden leaves?

Are you dreaming far ...

of a journey to the stars –
you and a friend on a flying carpet,
zooming way past Mars?

Are you dreaming deep ...

of holding an elephant's tail
then diving into the blue,
to swim by the side of a whale?

On the back seat of the car,
Joanna's sleeping tight.

What are you dreaming, Joanna,
as we travel through the night?

52

QUIET

Quiet as the night-time air
coming in off the sea.

Quiet as an owl's wings,
as it drops from a tree.

Quiet as the tread of a mouse
with midnight eyes.

Quiet as the stars in the great, wide
field of the skies.

Quiet as a leaf falling down
to the ground in a wood.

Sometimes a bit of quiet
can be good.

FOUR MOONS

The winter
moon is a silver
face, with a friendly
wink on a cold,
black night.

The spring moon is a magic egg, hatching a skyful of new moonshine.

The summer
moon is a ball
of straw – gold and
warm, and bright
as a smile.

The autumn
moon is a rosy
apple, ripe for
picking down from
the sky.

THE MIDDLE OF THE NIGHT

It's the middle of the night.

The knives and forks are asleep in the kitchen.
The towels are asleep in the bathroom.

The curtains are asleep in the windows.
The tiles are asleep on the rooftops.

The flowers are asleep in the gardens.
The train is asleep in the station.

The wind is asleep in the clouds.
But the stars are *awake* in the sky.

It's the middle of the middle of the night.

THE BAKER DOG

In the small of the night,
the whole town is still.

But the baker dog is up.
The baker dog is working.
A glow from his oven
warms the baker dog's face.

While we rest in bed,
he's measuring and mixing.

While we're fast asleep,
he's stirring and kneading.

While we're lost in dreams,
he bakes trays of bread.

In the small of the night,
everything is still.

But the baker dog is up.
The baker dog is working.
The baker dog is making
the town's morning bread.

A THOUSAND STARS

Look. A night of a thousand stars,

Among the stars,
a blue planet.

On the blue planet,
a quiet stretch of land.

Across the land,
the lights of sleeping cities.

Between the cities,
hills, valleys and fields,

On the edge of the fields,
a wood.

Off in the wood,
a tall tree.

On a branch of the tree,
an owl.

In the owl's eyes,
look. A night of a thousand stars.

CAVE BEAR'S SNORE

A witch can be quite nasty.
So can a crocodile's claw.
But nothing is as terrible as ...

a great big cave bear's snore!

A volcano's pretty scary.
So's a lion's roar.
But nothing is as terrible as ...

a great big cave bear's snore!

A smashing plate will shock you.
So will a slamming door.
You'll jump out of your skin if you hear
the snarl of a wild boar.

But go into a bear cave
and you'll find out, for sure ...
that nothing is as terrible,
as frightful or intolerable,
as horrible or abominable as ...

a great big cave bear's snore!

(Except for a great big cave bear waking up
and finding you in its cave...)

SOMETHING HAPPENS

Written with my hat raised to Robert Louis Stevenson for his poem
'The Land of Counterpane'. My mum used to read me that at bedtime.

Something happens
to your bed
when the light goes out
and you are falling asleep.

Grass starts to grow
on the hill of your pillow.
Then come the colours
of tiny wild flowers, too.

Where your covers
drop steeply down,
two small eagles
glide and circle in the air.

And down in the valley
where your arm curls,
a shoal of fish swims up
a hidden stream.

As soon as the first
light arrives, the grass,
the birds, the stream
and the fish disappear.

Your bed is just
pillows and covers.
But next time you sleep
something *else* will happen.

THE WORLD IS BUSY

In the morning, the world is busy

waking, stretching,
chatting, dressing,
yawning, thinking,
eating, drinking.

During the day, the world is busy

getting, going,
toing-froing,
giving, taking,
Joking, racing.

In the night, the world is busy

sleeping.

THANK YOUS:

With thanks to Rachel Rooney for casting
a poet's eye over an early draft of this book,
and sending back thoughts.
~ S. T.

Special thanks to my partner
who is always supportive and lovely.
And thank you to my special little babies
who are more inspiring to me than
anything else in the whole world.
~ A. A.

First published 2022 by Walker Books Ltd
87 Vauxhall Walk, London SE11 5HJ

2 4 6 8 10 9 7 5 3 1

Text © 2022 Sean Taylor
Illustrations © 2022 Anuska Allepuz
The right of Sean Taylor and Anuska Allepuz to be identified
as the author and illustrator respectively of this work has
been asserted in accordance with the Copyright, Designs
and Patents Act 1988

This book has been typeset in Intro book

Printed in China

All rights reserved. No part of this book may be reproduced,
transmitted or stored in an information retrieval system
in any form or by any means, graphic, electronic or mechanical,
including photocopying, taping and recording, without
prior written permission from the publisher.

British Library Cataloguing in Publication Data:
a catalogue record for this book is available
from the British Library

ISBN 978-1-4063-8790-2

www.walker.co.uk